The
WITCHES
of
BENEVENTO

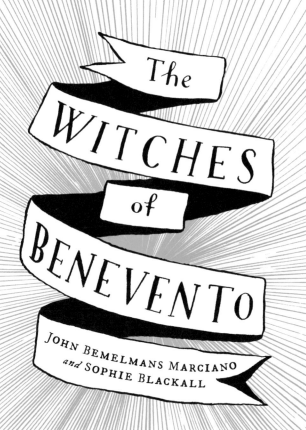

The WITCHES of BENEVENTO

JOHN BEMELMANS MARCIANO
and SOPHIE BLACKALL

THE ALL-POWERFUL RING

A Primo Story

VIKING

VIKING

An imprint of Penguin Random House LLC
375 Hudson Street
New York, New York 10014

First published in the United States of America by Viking,
an imprint of Penguin Random House LLC, 2016

LIBRARY OF CONGRESS CATALOGING-IN-PUBLICATION DATA IS AVAILABLE.
ISBN: 978-0-451-47180-2

1   3   5   7   9   10   8   6   4   2

Manufactured in China   Set in IM FELL French Canon
Book design by Nancy Brennan

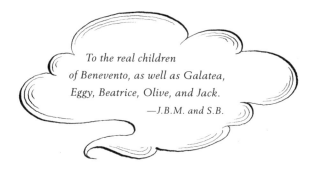

*To the real children
of Benevento, as well as Galatea,
Eggy, Beatrice, Olive, and Jack.*

—J.B.M. and S.B.

Emilio

Rosa

Primo

Maria Beppina

Sergio

CONTENTS

Dear Reader,

Welcome to the Triggio, that little neighborhood that lies in lowest Benevento. The dusty, noisy, dirty, smelly, run-down, rude, no-decent-person-DARE-go-there <u>Triggio</u>. Oh, how I love it!

Of course, I <u>am</u> a demon, and nowhere in Benevento are we witch-folk so welcomed as in the Triggio. All of my friends—be they spirits, fairies, ghosts, or the Clopper—love it here.

For the most part, we supernatural types cohabitate peacefully with our non-witch neighbors. Of course, we can't help but put a scare into you once in a while. None of us will really hurt you. None of us, that is, except the <u>Manalonga!</u>

Manalonga lurk under bridges and in wells just WAITING for the opportunity to reach their long arms up to grab someone and take them down to wherever it is they take their victims. Even WE are afraid of them. But you children—you are the ones the Long-Arms want the most!

Be careful, now—they'll say ANY-thing to trick you! They'll pretend to be your best friend or the boy you have a crush on or maybe your dad—anything it takes to get you to lean over the bridge or look down into the well. Then—SNATCH!

And unlike our friend the Clopper, the Manalonga actually have grabbed someone (or so the good folk of the Triggio believe). His name was Beppe Sfortunato, and he was a child who just happened to be walking over the bridge one day, not paying enough attention.

Beppe's family still lives in the Triggio, including the boy who would have been his nephew—a boy who is far TOO brave for his own good!

Is it wise to have such courage?

THE WITCHES
of
BENEVENTO

*When you hear the Clopper's **clop clop clop**,*

Run through the Theater and never stop.

Keep far from Bridges and from Wells,

Where Manalonga love to dwell.

If you are good and do your chores,

The Janara won't get you while you snore.

Respect your Ghosts and love your Sprites,

Kiss your Mom and say Good Night.

THE ALL-POWERFUL RING

A Primo Story

1

GUTS

CLANK clank clank! goes the mighty sword.

Or rather, *tik tik tik* goes the long, thick stick. Primo is just *saying* "**clank clank clank**."

"The glorious knight swings to behead the hideous monster!" he cries.

The hideous monster being his cousin Rosa.

Primo is with the Twins on what used to be the roof of their barn. He leaps from one beam to the next, daring Rosa to do the same. "Come and fight, you cowardly beast!" he says, and whacks her on the butt.

"That's **IT**, donkey-brains!" she says, throwing down a tile and leaping across beams to tackle him.

Primo fends Rosa off for a moment with his sword-stick, but then she grabs his leg and pulls him down. They wrestle on the thin— and *shaking*—rafters of the barn.

"You two are going to kill each other!" Rosa's twin, Emilio, says through the slats of the barn roof. "Or Father will. You guys are supposed to be laying tiles, not playing—remember?"

Rosa, grumbling, picks up a tile to get back to work, but when Primo says, "Yeah, stop messing around, little cousin!" she can't help but throw it at his head. Primo ducks, but the tile hits the barn wall and cracks at the very moment the Twins' father is hauling up another load of tiles.

Uncle Enzo looks up, furious, and pulls down his lower eyelid. His warning sign.

Primo sheepishly goes back to work. You don't mess with Uncle Enzo. *Ever.* And he's been even meaner than usual lately, because of the Janara.

It's shaping up to be the worst Janara season anyone can remember. Rosa and Emilio's farm has been wracked by witchy mischief for a week. The worst came last night, when all the tiles from the roof of the barn got blown off and tossed into the fields. It's like a tornado hit it!

Friends and neighbors are helping put the roof back together. The Twins' brother, Dino, and the other little kids are out in the fields, tracking down the tiles. Sergio is the only big kid with them. He's too afraid of heights to work on the roof, although he pretends that has nothing to do with it. Not Primo. Primo loves heights.

"Look, we need to do *something*," Primo says, taking a tile from the basket. "Forget hanging salt on the doorknobs and Zia Pia's spells and potions. We need to take matters into our own hands!"

"And how can we do that?" Emilio says.

Primo's answer: "Augurs."

"Otters?" Rosa says.

"No, *augurs*. That's what you call it when you slaughter an animal and read their guts," Primo says. "It's how the ancient Roman priests read the future, so it's got to be the best way!"

Although he states this as fact, Primo is half making up what he's saying as he goes along.

The first time Primo ever even heard of auguring was a few nights ago when Momma was making rabbit for dinner and Maria Beppina's dad started talking about it. It was pretty much the first interesting thing Uncle Tommaso ever said.

"The insides of animals hold all kinds of secrets," Primo says. "Like to everything!"

"Even if that's true, none of us knows the first thing about how to auger," Emilio says.

"Don't worry," Primo says, sticking his thumb in his own chest. **"I'll** know what I'm looking for when I see it."

A rumble of thunder sounds in the distance. "Is it going to rain?" Rosa says.

"No way," Primo says. "It's too sunny."

Creeping toward them across the sky are wispy black clouds that resemble the twirls of smoke coming out of nearby chimneys. All of a sudden, in spite of the sun, it starts to rain.

"I hope you're better at reading the guts of

animals than you are clouds," Rosa says. Primo sticks his tongue out at her, jumps off the side of the barn into a haystack, and starts running for home.

"Hey, wait up!" Sergio calls from the field, but Primo is already gone.

2
GET THAT EEL!

THERE'S an old saying in Benevento that a drop of rain on the roof of the castle becomes a river by the time it reaches the Triggio. Racing through the rain, Primo is heading upstream. Literally!

At his front door, Primo runs into Poppa. He is carrying a basket.

"What's in the basket?!" Primo yells above the thrum of the rain.

"You'll see!" Poppa yells back.

"Gather around, family, gather around," Poppa says when they get inside. "I have a surprise!"

Poppa always has surprises. Primo's older

sister, Isidora, and his grandmother Nonna Jovanna come to the table, ready to be thrilled. Momma, on the other hand, is only ready to be annoyed.

Father opens the basket to reveal—"Ta-**da**!"— an eel.

"An *eel*?" Momma says. "How can you spend our money on an eel? That's only for holidays and feast days!"

TA-DA!

"I didn't spend any money!" Poppa says. "I traded it for what Renzo the Barber owes at the vegetable stand. He'll never have the money to pay us, so at least we got *something.*"

This only makes Momma more angry—she can't stand Renzo. Or any of Poppa's friends. "If you made Renzo and the rest of those lay-abouts pay in silver coin instead of IOUs, then *we* wouldn't be half-starving all the time!"

"But tonight we have eel!" Poppa says. "And did I mention it's a *magic* eel?" He winks at Primo. "It will grant us three wishes!"

"You and your stupid jokes," Momma says, shaking her head. Then, to Primo: "Go tell your cousin to come help with dinner."

Primo rolls his eyes. Why does *he* always have to be the one to go upstairs and call Maria Beppina? And why does his cousin always have to eat with them? It's embarrassing enough that she and her strange father are related to him *and* live upstairs.

Kids like that jerk Mozzo make fun of Primo because of Maria Beppina. He always defends her, of course—she *is* his cousin—but why can't she be a little less strange herself?

Primo pushes the door out into the driving rain and takes the outside steps two at a time to the upper apartment. He bangs hard on the door. When Maria Beppina opens it, Primo says, "Dinner! Eel!" and runs back down as fast as he can.

Back inside, Momma is putting branches on the fire. "Too much, too much!" Nonna Jovanna

says. "You want to roast it, not burn it!"

"I know how to cook an eel, Mother!" Momma says. She gets out the cleaver to whack its head off. "Now please, open the basket."

Momma reaches in and grabs the eel. But the beast slithers out of her hands and curls up her arm. It lands on the floor with a **thud**.

"Body of Bacchus!" Momma says. The eel takes off.

Nonna Jovanna says, "I got it!"

But it goes right through her legs. "No, *I* have it!" Primo says, and dives under the table.

"It's here!" Isidora says, lifting a pot.

The front door opens. It's Maria Beppina. **"NO!"** everyone shouts as the eel slithers outside.

"Follow that EEL!"

The rain is coming down in sheets and the street now *is* a river, so much so that the eel can swim.

Down, through, up, and across the alleys of

the Triggio it goes. But at the Theater, the eel
vanishes. Everyone looks frantically in the gal-
leries and arches and behind rocks.

"**There!**" cries Isidora, pointing past Primo
to the street above the Theater. Primo's heart
leaps as he watches the eel slither right by him
and turn the corner out of sight. He takes off
after it, now in the eel-chasing lead.

On the other side of the Theater, Primo follows the eel to the courtyard in front of the Cemetery of Dead Babies. The eel slithers up the well in the center of it and comes to rest on its wide stone rim. The beast then turns its head to face Primo.

*Hello, Primo! I really **am** a magic eel. Come and grab me, dear boy, and I will grant you all the wishes you desire!*

Primo freezes. The voice isn't coming from the eel. It's coming from the well. *Inside* the well.

Manalonga!

What are you waiting for, Primo? Come get me!

COME GET ME!

"What are you waiting for, Primo?" his family yells from behind. "Go get it!"

GO GET IT!

In that instant, the eel turns and slithers down the well. Primo races to its edge and peers down into the darkness.

BOOM!

A flash of lightning brightens the inside of the well for an instant, and that's when Primo sees it. *Something,* hurtling up toward him, reaching for him. Is it a hand? The hand of a Manalonga?

Primo launches himself back and away, banging into his sister and bringing them both tumbling down into a puddle, right as the rest of the family arrives.

"You stupid toad!" Isidora says to Primo. "Why didn't you grab it when you had the chance!"

"Well, why did Maria Beppina have to open the door?" Primo says.

"There goes our money, right down a long dark hole, like it always does!" Momma says, throwing her hands up in the air.

"Well, why didn't you hold on to it!" Poppa says to Momma.

"So it's *my* fault you let your deadbeat friends take whatever they want and…"

3

THE TALE OF
BEPPE SFORTUNATO

⟨ornament⟩

DID I really see what I think I saw?

Everyone else has gone to sleep, but the question won't stop banging around Primo's head. Staring at the goddess Diana (the half an ancient marble head that sits in their kitchen wall), Primo tries to bring the moment back.

It all happened so fast—as fast as the flash of lightning itself—but that *hand!* It was a hand, wasn't it? A green scaly hand with long claw-like fingers. Now he can *see* it, right there in his head!

The only kid Primo knows who has seen the hand of a Manalonga is Rosa. This happened because she didn't do a very simple thing, which every mother in Benevento tells every kid from the time they are a baby.

Whenever you need to use a well
Kiss a pebble and speak this spell:
Soul, Sun, Stars, Sky,
Manalonga say good-bye!

One day, Rosa somehow forgot to kiss the pebble and got dragged halfway down her family's well. She only escaped, she claims, because she beat the Manalonga off with her pail.

Not that Primo believes Rosa—not about the beating-off-the-Manalonga part, anyway—but can he believe himself? Still, when he thinks about that green scaly hand, coming up, trying to grab him, he feels the prickles of fear all over again.

Primo *hates* being afraid. Of anything. Other kids, like Maria Beppina, are scared of witches. She's even terrified of the Clopper catching her, although everyone knows that weird old witch has never caught anyone.

Primo laughs at all that stuff, but he can't laugh at the Manalonga. Then again, *no one* laughs at the Manalonga.

Manalonga lurk underwater and underground, just waiting for the chance to trick you into coming near so they can snatch you.

Avoiding them in wells is easy enough. Bridges are more dangerous. The best you can do is stick to the middle path—the safety zone—and plug your ears with your fingers and sing *LA-la-la-la-LA!* as loud as you can. And run!

Where do Manalonga take their victims? Some say it's to the Underworld, but Nonna Jovanna says it's to caves that are so dark they pluck out your eyes because you won't need them anymore, and they set you to work mining for silver. No one knows for sure, and it's the not-knowing that's the scariest part.

Actually, the *scariest* part is that—unlike the Clopper—a Manalonga **has** caught somebody: Beppe Sfortunato.

Everyone in the Triggio knows of the day a Manalonga snatched Beppe Sfortunato. To Primo, however, the story means something extra, because Beppe is Primo's uncle. Or would have been, if he hadn't got gotten.

Beppe was the older brother of Primo's mom. Nonna Jovanna always says how Primo is just like Beppe—never doing what he's told, always looking for adventure.

"You have a special destiny, Primo, just like my Beppe," she says. "But yours will turn out as well as his did badly!"

The one thing Nonna Jovanna and his mom never talk about is the day Beppe got snatched. But Poppa does.

"That's the stone—right *there*—where Beppe was standing," Poppa would always say when they crossed the bridge. He would doff his cap. "And I was back over there, on the road, watching everything.

"We were your age, Beppe and I, when it happened. It was a day like any other, a day like today." Poppa would say this if it was sunny, and sometimes even if it was rainy.

"Beppe was walking over the bridge out of town to the fields when he heard the voice. It was the voice of Matalena—the prettiest, sweetest girl in town. I could hear it, too, as clear as you can hear me right now.

"'Beppe! Beppe!' the voice called from beneath

the bridge. 'Look at this beautiful bottle I found! I think it has a message inside, but I can't get it out! Can you come help me?'

"'Beppe, no!' I shouted. But it was too late. He couldn't help himself. He walked to the edge of the bridge, leaned over, and WHOP!" Poppa would snatch at the air with his fist. "The Manalonga got him."

Poppa would put his old red cap back on and take a deep breath.

"Oh, I remember that terrible shriek, the horrible claws on the monster's hands, and the sickening splash when Beppe was pulled into the water.

"Everyone in the Triggio went searching the water for Beppe, but there was nothing. No Beppe, no Manalonga. Even the fish were gone."

"But how did you *hear* the Manalonga?" Primo would ask. Only the person being called to is supposed to be able to hear the voice of a Manalonga.

BEPPE!

BEPPE!

BEPPE!

PPE!

Poppa would shrug. "I heard what I heard!"

It's a mystery, but so is everything about the Manalonga. There is no understanding them.

Or is there? Maybe that eel was a sign. "Augurs!" Primo says to Diana, snapping his fingers.

He has an idea, a great idea, but he needs help. Maria Beppina's help.

4
LAUNDRY DAY

PRIMO loves Tuesday afternoons. Laundry day! It's not that Primo likes doing the wash—in fact, he hates that part, and he avoids it at all costs. He likes laundry day because he gets to hang out with his cousins at the river rather than be stuck up at the boring grocery stand.

This laundry day is going to be special, however. Primo can hardly keep in all he has to say when he gets to the river.

The Twins are talking about the latest round of Janara mischief to hit their farm, something about bees chasing them.

"Ah, that's nothing!" Primo says. "You won't believe what happened to *me* last night!"

Primo tells the Twins about the eel escaping and luring him to the well and how the Manalonga pretended to be the eel. "And then, I saw"—he leans in and lowers his voice—"*it*! A Manalonga! It reached its hand out of the well and tried to grab me!" He is now sure that it did.

The Twins are both impressed that he has seen a Manalonga, although of course Rosa has to tell *her* story about beating one off with a bucket.

"But the eel! The *eel* is what's important," Primo says. "The eel is a sign!"

"It does sound like a sign," Emilio admits. He stops washing the shirt he is holding in the river. "Did you ask Nonna Jovanna about it?"

"She said it was the biggest sign ever!" Actually, she said it was the *worst* sign ever, but what's the difference? Primo keeps talking. "It's proof that animals give signs and that if we augur one—like a fish—we can solve your Janara problem for sure."

"A runaway eel doesn't prove that at all!" Emilio says. "And you don't—"

"I know what you're going to say," Primo says, cutting off Emilio. "*You don't know the first thing about auguring!* Well, now I do, because I read all about it. In a **book**!"

"But you don't know how to read, donkeybrains!" Rosa says.

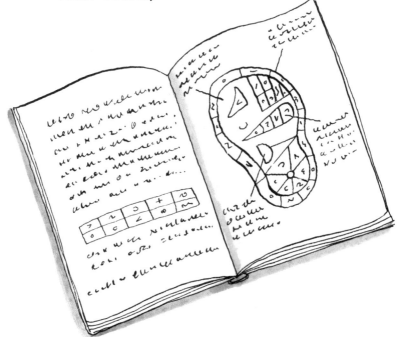

"Well, *I* didn't read it. Maria Beppina did," Primo says, turning to his cousin. "I went up to her apartment this morning to look through her dad's books. Isn't that right, Maria Beppina?"

"Well, we *did* read about auguring," Maria Beppina says sheepishly. "And it *was* in a book."

There is nothing more the Twins can say. If they read about it in a *book*, well, they must know what they're doing. Emilio is impressed by anything that comes from a book.

The thing is, Uncle Tommaso's books only told them what auguring *is*, not how to actually do it. But Primo isn't going to let this fact ruin his very smart idea of looking in a book in the first place.

"All we have to do is catch a fish, gut it, and then—"

"Stop bothering your friends and start washing, you little toad!" Isidora hollers at Primo from across the river.

Why does his sister always have to nag? She used to be fun, but about six months ago she began to act all moody and weird. Poppa says girls get like that when they turn twelve and you just need to stay out of their way. The problem is that Isidora is *always* in Primo's way.

"Start washing, I said!" she repeats.

"In a minute, in a minute!" Primo yells back, although he has no intention of helping.

Auguring is *way* more important than doing laundry.

START WASHING!

To get started, Primo makes a hook out of some wire and attaches it to a line. He then looks under rocks for a worm, skewers one on his hook, and lowers it into the water.

Rosa, thinking that auguring is as good an idea as any (and never one to do work instead of have fun), finds an old pole on the bank of the river and—borrowing a knife from one of Emilio's pockets— sharpens it into a spear. She then takes jabs at the water, loudly splashing.

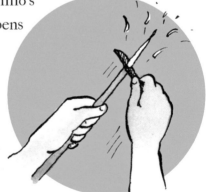

"Hah! You'll never get one *that* way!" Primo says, carefully lowering and raising his line and hook.

"This auguring is the stupidest idea I ever heard of," Isidora says. "You can't tell anything about a Janara from the insides of a fish!"

"Like *you* know anything about Janara!" Primo says.

"I know more than you think," Isidora mutters under her breath. She then grabs a basket of wet clothes and walks off. "Do that other basket or *you* answer to Momma!" she calls back over her shoulder.

OR YOU ANSWER TO MOMMA!

"Oh, I *had* that one!" Primo says, with every near miss being an even nearer near miss. "And *that* one! Dang!"

"Got one!" Rosa shouts. She lifts her spear triumphantly, fish flapping.

"Lucky stab," Primo grumbles. "It's so big you couldn't have missed it."

Anxious to get started, Primo goes to pull the fish off the spear. Rosa, however, raises it *just* out of his reach and laughs. And then again.

"Come *on*, Rosa!" Primo says.

Finally allowed to grab it, Primo puts the poor creature out of its misery with Emilio's knife. He then slices the fish open

like he's done a hundred times with Poppa, but he isn't quite sure where to go next. The stomach seems like as good a place to start as any, so he cuts it open.

Something falls out.
Something shiny.

"Is that a fishhook?" Rosa asks.

"This is *no* fishhook," Primo says, picking it up. "It's a ring!" He rubs it against his shirt and holds it to the sun.

"A *gold* ring!" Emilio says.

In the next minute, Sergio and Maria Beppina are huddled around them, too, oohing and ahhing.

"See, I knew it! I *told* you guys I'd find something important!" Primo says, even

though he's as surprised as any of them.

"Who do you think it belongs to?" Rosa says. "The governor's wife? A queen?"

"I don't think there are any queens around here," Maria Beppina says.

"Well, it's way too fancy for any Triggio dweller, that's for sure," Sergio says. "It must come from someone up the hill."

"Or upriver," says Emilio. "That fish could have swum from anywhere."

"No, guys—don't you see? It's not the ring of a *person*," Primo says, an amazing idea dawning on him. "It's the ring of a Manalonga! It must have fallen off when one of them was trying to snatch a kid. And then this fish gobbled it up."

"I never heard of Manalonga having rings," Emilio says.

"Yeah, I don't remember seeing one on ours," Rosa adds. But after Sergio says he thinks he heard something about Manalonga and rings, Rosa says, "Oh yeah, I think I *did* see a ring."

"Manalonga are *famous* for having rings," Primo says, trying to convince himself as much as anyone. "The one I saw at the well yesterday definitely had one."

Rosa touches the ring. "I don't know if it's from a Manalonga or what," she says. "But it sure is pretty."

"Pretty, *phooey!* **Powerful** is what it is!" Primo says, snatching it away. "Can't you feel the power coming off of it? It's like heat."

The others keep talking, none of them quite convinced the ring is really so powerful, let alone that it belonged to a Manalonga. Primo can hardly hear them, though. The loudest voice in his head is his own, saying over and over:

THIS IS THE MOST AMAZING THING THAT EVER HAPPENED!

5
DESTINY

"I must have quiet."

The voice of Zia Pia is always spooky, just like her home. A weak oil lamp gives off barely enough light to see and casts long shadows everywhere.

"*Quiet . . .*" she repeats, closing her eyes and moving her hand in circles above a pitcher.

"Can you stop *breathing* so loud?" Primo whispers to Maria Beppina.

"*Sorry,*" his cousin says softly, turning red. She tries to breathe less loudly—or stop altogether—but after outrunning the Clopper and climbing Zia Pia's stairs, she can't help herself.

"*Assa . . . massa . . . pissa . . . **harissa**!*"

Zia Pia speaks her spell like a moan and rubs the air with a turned-down palm.

Primo can feel the magic working. He is glad he dragged the others here again—Zia Pia will *convince* them how powerful the ring is!

The old fortune-teller opens her eyes and pours water from the pitcher into a wide-mouthed bowl she has placed in front of herself. She lifts the ring above the water. "*Arissa, fiyo, kayo!*" she says and lets the ring fall—*dop!*—into the water.

Zia Pia now lifts the smoking lamp and begins searching for images in the gentle ripples of the water.

"Mmm, *mmm*," she says.

"What is it?" Primo says. "Do you see some-thing?" Primo thinks he can make out the arm of a Manalonga. Or is it a Janara flying?

"*Mmmm*," Zia Pia says again.

"What do you see?"

"What do I see?" Zia Pia says. "I see nothing."

"Nothing?" Primo says. "How can you see *nothing*?"

"Well I see *everything*," the fortune-teller says. "The entire *spirit* world I see. But of this ring?" She pulls it out of the water. "Nothing."

Primo looks down into the bowl. The water is now still. "Are you sure this thing is working?"

"My silly boy, this ring is nothing but a trin-ket!" Zia Pia says, pinching Primo's cheek.

"But I can read disappointment in your cute face as surely as I can read the great beyond, and I can't stand it. I tell you what I will do. I will *buy* this ring from you. After all, I *do* love trinkets." She wiggles her fingers, thick with jeweled rings. "Maybe I will give you . . . twelve quattrini?"

"A dozen lousy coppers?" Primo says.

"Fine, one silver scudo," Zia Pia says, as if she is being too generous. "But that is my final offer!"

"No way!" Primo says, swiping the ring out of her hand. "I'm a kid, not an idiot!"

"*Two* scudi!" The voice of Zia Pia follows them down the stairs. "But *that* is my final offer!"

"She was lying to us!" Primo says when they are down in the Theater. "She saw the ring's power! That's why she wanted it for herself—that's PROOF of how powerful this ring is!"

"Or that it's worth something. It is *gold*, after all," Emilio says. "At least I think it is."

Primo shakes his head. "That's not the reason," he says. "That

TWO SCUDI!

old fortune-teller wants it because it's the ring of a Manalonga. I'm sure of it!"

"But how can you be *sure*?" Emilio says. "You're just guessing!"

"I was right about the auguring, wasn't I?" Primo says.

"Even a blind hog finds an acorn once in a while," Rosa says.

"Look, guys, I don't know about the ring, but I know I have to go give my ghost his offering," Sergio says. "He'll yell at me if I'm late again."

The Twins leave for home also, and then Maria Beppina tells Primo she has to go, too.

"I believe you, Primo," Maria Beppina says. "A ring like that *has* to be magical."

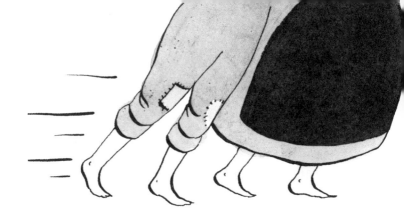

What Maria Beppina thinks is no consolation—she always says what Primo wants to hear. It's the *others* he needs to believe him!

With nothing to do but head to work, Primo walks up to the vegetable stand alone, disappointed and thrilled. How can you be both?

Taking the fishing line out of his pocket, Primo tosses away the hook. He then threads the string through the ring and ties the line around his neck, creating an amulet. That done, Primo tucks the dangling ring inside his shirt lest someone try to steal it, or—more likely— his mom make him sell it.

Primo knows this ring is the most amazing thing ever—the destiny he's been waiting for. The only problem is he has no idea what to *do* with it.

At the stand, the last customer of the day is Amerigo Pegleg, as usual. He roots through what bunches of withered greens are left, the stuff Primo would otherwise throw away.

"Feels like a real Janara night's a-coming, boy," Amerigo says, looking up at the darkening sky with a smile. "They'll be swarming 'round the old walnut tree tonight!"

The Tree of the Janara! *That's **it***, Primo thinks.

The Tree of the Janara is the place where witches gather before going out for a night of mischiefing. It's a couple of hours' walk upriver, next to the Bridge of Ancient Ages. Primo doesn't know anyone who's ever gone to the Tree, at least not at night.

Of course, no one leaves town after dark on account of all the bandits and wild animals. Primo isn't afraid, however. Not with the ring— *this* ring.

Primo imagines exactly how it will go: In the middle of the night, after a long walk, he and the others will arrive at the Bridge just as the demons are stirring their cauldrons and the Janara are swarming around the Tree. When the witches see them, they will swoop like hawks for the kill. As his cousins and Sergio cower, Primo will pull out the ring and the Janara will flee in terror.

Maybe the ring is *so* powerful he will be able

to catch a Janara by the hair. Imagine *that*! Nonna Jovanna says if you capture a Janara, your family gets seven generations of good fortune!

As night falls, Primo locks up the stand. He then takes the ring out from his shirt and holds it in the moonlight.

A trinket, Zia Pia said! Primo will show her—show everyone—the true power of the ring! The *all*-powerful ring!

6

A VERY LONG NIGHT

WAITING.

Why does Primo always have to wait for everything? Waiting is never fun, but it's the worst when you are waiting for something really important.

From his perch up in the tree—the Tree of the Janara!—Primo looks up at the stars and moon, trying to judge how far across the sky they've wheeled. It must be midnight. So where are the Janara?

The others had no faith. Or patience. They all left as soon as they got here and saw there weren't any Janara. Well, all of them except the one he *most* wishes had left.

Sitting in a different tree—a walnut tree—is Rosa. She believes that *her* tree is the Tree of the Janara.

She could **not** be more wrong. Which tree is the witch tree is *so* obvious. His tree looks just the way Primo always pictured it, standing right beside the Bridge of Ancient Ages.

Rosa's tree, on the other hand, isn't even *close* to the bridge, but that doesn't stop her from insisting she's sitting in the right one. Which is just like her. You could tell her the sky is blue and she'd swear it's green. It drives Primo crazy!

THIS WAS YOUR DUMBEST IDEA EVER!

He can't even *look* at her sitting in that stupid tree, let alone speak to her. Primo will get the last laugh, however, when the Janara come and start flying around *his* tree.

But when will they get here? Primo is willing to stay up here all night if he has to, but how much longer will the Janara make him wait? As the moon and stars wheel farther and farther across the black sky, Primo begins to get mad at the Janara, like their not coming is a mischief they are playing on him.

"This was your dumbest idea ever!" Rosa says, breaking the silence. "What made you think the Janara would actually come here, anyway?"

"What do you mean? Everyone knows this is where they come!" Primo says. Then he snaps his fingers. "Hey, I know why they aren't here!"

"Why?"

"The ring!" Primo says. "It's *so* powerful it scared them off! They must be able to feel its magic from **miles** away!"

"Ah, *fiddlesticks*!" Rosa says. "Zia Pia's right! That ring is nothing but a trinket!"

"*Hmph!*" Primo says, and goes back to giving her the silent treatment.

After a while, Rosa yawns, and Primo can't help yawning himself. And again. It is getting *so* late and Primo is *so* tired, he just wishes he could sleep. He tries to fight it off, but then he loses track of his thoughts, and his thoughts drift into dreams, and now he *is* face-to-face with a Janara, and the weird thing is she looks just like his sister, and . . . and . . .

He feels something hit him. He wakes up.

"HA! You fell asleep!" Rosa says, and fires another walnut at him.

"Did not!" Primo says, ducking the flying nut.

"Did too!" Rosa says and nails him, right on the kneecap.

"**OW**!" Primo yelps.

"Primo the dreamer,
Primo the schemer,
Hit him with a walnut
And Primo's a screamer!"

Rosa is so proud of her rhyme that she chants it over and over again.

And over again.

This is going to be a loooong night, but Primo will NOT fall asleep again.

Primo falls asleep again. This is how he wakes up:

"Primo! Primo!"

Primo feels himself being shaken.

"Primo! Primo!"

"What *is* it?"

"Primo, you have to go look at yourself!" Rosa says. "Go to the river!"

Primo is in the tree and—seeing the barest glow of dawn to the east—realizes he must have slept half the night away.

"Why do I have to go look at myself?"

"Don't you *feel* something different on your head?" Rosa says, standing on the ground below Primo.

He does! Feel something different, that is.

"What is it?" he says.

"Proof that the Janara came while you were sleeping, that's what!" Rosa says, excited. "Go look in the river and see!"

Primo practically kills himself hurrying-scurrying down the tree and then the steep bank to the muddy riverbed. Gazing down into the brown mirror of the water, Primo sees what's on his head: Rosa's head scarf.

"It was a mischief!" Rosa says.

Primo can't believe it, except of course he can! He *knew* the Janara would come and is so *mad* he missed them, and he *can't* believe they

played an actual mischief on him and . . . and . . .

"Why are you laughing?" he asks Rosa, who is doubled over.

"The Janara never came, donkey-brains! You were so fast asleep I put my head scarf on you. You look like your *grandma*!" She snickers.

Primo rips the thing off and throws it into the river.

"Hey, you big jerk!" Rosa says as it floats downstream. She jumps into the river and chases after it, grabbing the cloth as it gets caught on some reeds.

Primo is already walking home.

7

A CHAPTER IN WHICH NOTHING GOES PRIMO'S WAY

THE whole way back, Primo has to listen to Rosa making fun of him and singing her stupid rhyme. He walks as fast as he can and still it's so late by the time he gets to his house that he has to go right to work.

"I don't even get to have breakfast?" Primo says.

"If you wanted food, you should have eaten at your cousins'!" Momma says, believing he spent the night at the Twins'.

At the stand, Primo is so tired he lies down under the table with the dried figs and honey on it and goes to sleep. A customer has to wake him up. Then Poppa comes and tells him he has to go all the way to Vipera to pick up three bar-rels of olive oil from the olive-presser there.

"Why can't Isidora go?" Primo says.

"She has to weave," Poppa says.

(Isidora has fingers like lightning, and her weaving makes the family twice as much money as what Poppa and Primo make at the stand.)

They don't own a mule or a cart, so they have to rent one from the Carrozzos. Everyone hates the Carrozzos. They're the richest family in the Triggio, and they make sure everyone knows it. The youngest boy, Mozzo, is the worst, a brat and a total know-it-all.

"You've got to hold a tight rein with this mule," Mozzo tells Primo while the fathers do business.

"Okay, okay," Primo

says, tired of hearing him explain *every* little thing. Like Primo doesn't know how to work a mule cart!

"And the brake on this wagon can stick . . ."

Primo exits the city through the Arch of Trajan and turns down toward the Ponticello, a tiny bridge that goes over a stream.

He thinks about testing the power of the ring. Shouldn't it protect him from the Manalonga who lives under the Ponticello? It must be a small Manalonga, since the bridge is so little. What if Primo doesn't stick his fingers in his ears and make noise?

As soon as the cart hits the bridge, however, Primo finds himself chanting *LA-la-la-la-LA!* at the top of his lungs.

LA-LA-LA-LA-LA

The whole long ride to Vipera, Primo can't stop thinking about two things: the ring, and how humiliating the whole trip to the Tree of the Janara was. He can't bear the thought of seeing any of his cousins today, which is one good thing about being sent out of town.

It is well past noon by the time Primo gets to Vipera, and when he does, he finds out it would have been better had he not come at all.

"We have no oil left!" the olive-presser says. "The Janara spilled out our last ten barrels."

The olive-presser's wife feels bad for Primo and gives him a nice bowl of fava-and-dandelion soup.

Back on the road, his full

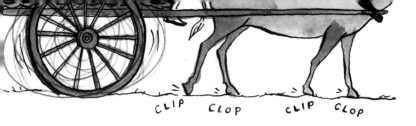

CLIP   CLOP   CLIP   CLOP

belly makes Primo sleepy again. With the swaying of the cart and the rhythm of clopping hooves, he can barely keep his eyes open. Of course, the mule knows the way home, and it won't hurt if Primo shuts his eyes for *just* a minute.

He wakes up to the sound of Rosa's voice.

Primo the dreamer,
Primo the schemer,
Hit him with a walnut
And Primo's a screamer!

"Shut **UP**!" Primo yells. Then he opens his eyes and sees where he is.

The mule
made it nearly all
the way back to town, but
stopped at the Ponticello. Instead of going over
the little bridge, however, the animal climbed
down to the grassy banks of the stream for a
snack.

Primo the dreamer . . . The sound of Rosa's
taunting—it's echoing out of the dark tunnel
under the bridge. But it can't be Rosa.

It's a Manalonga!

Terrified, Primo hops off the seat of the
wagon, jumps across the stream, and yanks on
the mule's bridle as hard as he can to get the
beast to go forward.

Meanwhile, the Manalonga keeps chanting.

...HIT HIM WITH A WALNUT...

Hit him with a walnut . . .

The black hole under the bridge—it's too far for the Manalonga to reach him, right? *Right?*

"Come on, you dummy! Come on!" Primo yells at the mule, pulling so hard it feels like his arms are coming out of their sockets. Finally, the animal rears its head up and Primo is able to get the mule to come charging up the hill.

Thank you, thank you! Primo thinks. Maybe the ring *is* good luck. After all, he was lying asleep right next to a Manalonga, and he survived. Maybe he shouldn't have been scared at all. Maybe—

CRACK!

The rear wheel of the cart hits a rock in the stream bank and snaps a wooden spoke.

Oh, *no*!

Returning the cart is even worse than Primo fears. "It's going to cost more than a scudo for the wheelwright to fix this!" Mozzo says, smiling. "How could you be so ***stupid***?"

Their fathers, meanwhile, barter and bicker over how much is owed on the repair. Hands and gestures fly. On the way out, Poppa smacks Primo—*thwack!*—on the back of the head.

Primo skips dinner and goes right to bed. He doesn't want to hear Momma complain about how much money the wheel cost, and he *really* doesn't want to explain to Maria Beppina what happened at the Tree. Knowing Rosa, of course, she probably told everybody everything and even made up *more* humiliating stuff that isn't true.

Which is why he has to grit his teeth when Rosa and Dino pull up in the delivery cart at the stand the next morning.

"I don't know why you even bother coming," Primo says. "You haven't had anything decent to sell since the mischiefs started."

"Well, we do now!" Rosa says, and pulls three crates of eggs off the cart. "There's lots more stuff, too."

"What happened?" Primo asks, surprised at how much she has to sell.

"I stopped the mischiefs, that's what happened!" Rosa says.

"*You* stopped them?" Primo says. "How?"

"With drawings of spirit dogs and a very special spell that I made up myself," Rosa says proudly. "It was even better than the rhyme I made up about *you*."

Primo doesn't believe for a moment that Rosa figured out how to beat the Janara. The annoying part is, *she* believes it.

All day at the stand Primo broods. He takes out the ring every time he is alone to look at it. Is it possible it *isn't* magic? No, it has to be! This ring is the MOST AMAZING THING to

ever happen. It was destiny to find the ring inside that fish—Primo's destiny! He's just got to prove it.

That's when another great idea hits him. If Uncle Tommaso's books talk about auguring, then they *must* have stuff about magic rings. Some of his books have pictures of ancient buildings and statues and jewelry—maybe one of them matches the ring.

This time, though, he isn't going to leave it to Maria Beppina to look through the books. No, her dad is the one who knows this stuff, so Primo is going to have his cousin show Uncle Tommaso the ring so *he* can look in the books and figure out what it is.

Primo goes up the stairs to Maria Beppina's apartment and takes the ring off the string around his neck. Before knocking on the door, he pauses. He looks at the ring in his hand. Should he *really* risk letting someone else have it? Especially his dopey cousin who is always messing things up? But Primo *has* to find out.

He knocks.

8
GOTTEN!

PRIMO wakes up anxious to see Maria Beppina and find out what her father learned about the ring, but Poppa is waiting at breakfast with an early morning mission.

"*Six, fourteen, ninety-eight,*" Poppa whispers to Primo so Momma can't hear, and palms him three quattrini. He then shoos Primo out the door.

Primo runs to the Inn at the Fork. "Six, fourteen, ninety-eight," he repeats to Bardo the tavern-keeper, handing him the coins.

While Bardo fills out a lottery ticket, Primo watches one of the turnspit dogs run in the wheel that spins meat over the fire. The other dog is sleeping, exhausted. Primo always feels bad for them, running but never getting anywhere, with that delicious-smelling food just out of reach.

On his way to the stand, Primo runs into the Twins.

"Father is so happy the mischiefs are over that he gave us the day off!" Rosa says.

"Let's play storm-the-castle!" Emilio says. "We'll meet you on the wall by the watchtower at the midday bell. I'll tell Sergio and Maria Beppina!"

Primo closes the stand early for lunch and is up on the wall by the first noon bell, but where are the others?

BONG *bong!* BONG *bong!* The second noon bell tolls.

They should all be here by now! What could be keeping them? That is when the terrible thought hits Primo: What if the others are late because Maria Beppina lost the ring and they are looking for it?

Primo *knew* he should never have given her the ring! That dumb Maria Beppina probably dropped the ring somewhere and now it's gone forever! He'll never forgive her!

Pacing, pacing the top of the walls, Primo gets more and more upset. Then he spots the Twins and Sergio, tearing through the city gate, running toward him and screaming. And *no* Maria Beppina!

"It was the Clopper!" one of them yells.

"We waited and waited for her, but she never came back!" another shouts.

"It's horrible! Horrible!"

"Wait!" Primo says. "What are you guys *talking* about??"

"The Clopper!" Rosa calls up. "The Clopper **got** Maria Beppina!"

Primo practically loses his balance and falls off the wall. He is sick with worry—not about his cousin, but about the ring!

Primo takes the circular stairs of the watchtower in three-step leaps until he is down with the others.

"What *happened*?" he asks.

"We were heading across the Theater and I was in the lead," Rosa says.

"Yeah, but Maria Beppina was right behind *me*!" Sergio says. "I was running and I heard the Clopper—she was louder than **ever**—and I looked back at Maria Beppina and I saw this scared look in her eyes. It was like she was saying, *Help me!*"

"And *I* was already on the other side and I looked back and Maria Beppina was **gone**!" Rosa says.

"We searched all around the Theater," Emilio says. "There was no sign of her. Anywhere!"

"The Clopper **got** her!" Rosa says again.

"But the Clopper's never gotten anyone!" Primo says.

"That's probably what they said when your Uncle Beppe got snatched," Rosa says. "Hey, wait—you know what is *so* weird? **Bepp**e, Maria **Bepp**ina—it's like they have the same name!"

"OH, NO, you're *right*!" Sergio says. "What are we going to do!?"

"The question is what is the *Clopper* going to do?" Rosa says. "To Maria Beppina!"

"Doesn't she eat kids?" Sergio says.

"That's what Nonna Jovanna says," Emilio says.

"Poor Maria Beppina!" Sergio says.

"I always liked her . . . " Rosa says, taking off her head scarf.

"Look, you don't know if she's dead. You don't even know if she got caught for sure!" Primo says. "It'd be just like Maria Beppina to chicken out and turn around for home."

"Home!" Rosa says. "We need to go check!"

But back at Maria Beppina and Primo's house they just find Primo's older sister, Isidora, weaving in the street outside the front door.

"I haven't seen her, but don't worry," Isidora says. "The Clopper is just some crazy old lady who's never hurt anybody! I'm sure Maria Beppina is fine."

But none of the kids believe it. At least, not until they see Maria Beppina walking home with their own eyes.

9
THE TALE OF MARIA BEPPINA

~ℚ~

THE Twins and Sergio crowd and hug Maria Beppina. Primo is relieved to see her wearing the ring! *Phew!*

"What happened? What happened?" they ask.

"It was . . ." Maria Beppina says, and pauses. Her hair and clothes are disheveled. "It was the **Clopper**! She got me!"

"No!"

"Wow!"

"Unreal!"

"How?"

Maria Beppina begins to stutter and sputter, like she is confused, unsure of what to say.

"I stopped!" she finally blurts out.

"You **stopped**?" Rosa says.

"On purpose?" Emilio says.

"That's the bravest thing I ever heard of!" Sergio says.

"Why would you *stop*?" Primo asks.

"To see what would happen," Maria Beppina says. "And what happened was . . ." She looks at all their faces. "It was *terrible*!"

The other kids stand there stunned, their mouths open.

"The Clopper grabbed me and dragged me down to her underground lair," Maria Beppina says. "And then she locked me in a rusty cage and started a fire under a giant pot. There were three hideous demons helping her and they were all starving hungry! They talked this crazy language that I couldn't understand, but I could tell they were going to boil me!"

"I don't know if I can hear any more!" Sergio says, looking sick.

"No, **more**!" Rosa says.

"The Clopper kept laughing this horrible laugh and calling me *dearie* and *sweetie* and telling me how nice it was to have a child to eat after all these years."

"This is amazing!"

"Amazing!"

"It's not just amazing," Rosa says. "It's the MOST AMAZING THING THAT EVER HAPPENED!"

Primo's ears—his whole face—burn. This *can't* be! Maria Beppina getting caught can't be the most amazing thing to ever happen, because the *ring* is the most amazing thing to ever happen!

Besides, *he* was supposed to be the hero! Not Maria Beppina! And not while wearing his ring!

But wait—the ring! That must be what saved her.

While the other kids pelt Maria Beppina with questions about how she escaped, Primo butts in with the answer.

"It was the ring!" says Primo, "Don't you guys see? The ring *protected* her from the Clopper."

"Is it true?" the other kids say, turning back to Maria Beppina.

Maria Beppina hesitates for a moment, as if she isn't sure what to say.

"Yes," Maria Beppina says at last. "Yes, it *is* true. The ring even started to **glow**."

"Whoa!"

"And *then* what?"

"The light from the ring blinded the Clopper and she had to blink and cover her eyes," Maria Beppina says, putting a hand over her own eyes.

"*Curse you, you little brat!* she said. *It was going to be a feast day for me!* It was like the ring was burning her, and the farther out I held it the more it hurt. *Fine! Fine! I'll let you out!* she screamed. *Just take that ring away from me!*"

Maria Beppina shrugs. "I actually felt kind of bad for her as I left."

"Wow, it's true!" Sergio says. "The ring *is* powerful!"

Even the Twins have to agree.

"I didn't believe it," Emilio says. "But you were right, Primo."

But being right isn't enough. Not for Primo. He has to *do* something. Something amazing.

10

TO DARE A MANALONGA

IT all makes sense now to Primo. The ring *did* keep the Janara away from the Bridge of Ancient Ages, and it was the reason the Manalonga at the Ponticello didn't dare do anything but make fun of him. The ring has as much power as Primo imagined—and more! Now Primo is finally going to do something with it. After all, he can't let Maria Beppina have all the glory.

"Where are you going, Primo?" Emilio asks.

"What are we doing?" Sergio says.

The other kids are following Primo on the path out of the city gate.

"What are you up to now, toad?" says Isidora, who can't help but come along, too.

"You'll see," Primo says.

When they get to the bridge, the other kids are ready to stick their fingers in their ears and run across it, but Primo holds up his hand.

"Wait."

They all look at him quizzically.

"Give me the ring," Primo says to Maria Beppina.

She does.

"I'm going to walk up the bridge and I'm going to *stay* on the bridge," Primo says. "In fact, I am going to stand on the exact spot where Uncle Beppe got snatched. And I'm going to *talk* to a Manalonga."

"What are you?" Isidora says. *"Crazy?"*

As the other kids plead with him to stop, Primo walks forward, climbing the ramp of the bridge. Alone.

"Don't be stupid, little brother!" Isidora calls after him.

"Yeah, come back, Primo!" Rosa says. "You don't have to prove yourself!"

Near the peak of the bridge, Primo stops and stands in the middle of it, three steps from either edge. The safety zone.

Primo feels his nerves, and then turns to the side wall of the bridge. His father always says:

> *That's the stone—right there—where Beppe was standing.*

He looks at it.

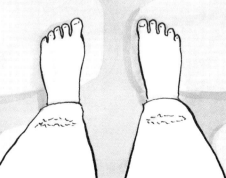

"Primo, no!" Isidora shouts.

He takes one step forward. The rushing water from beneath grows louder. Slowly, it forms into a voice.

Primo, the voice calls. *How are you, Primo?*

It isn't like any other time he's heard the voice. He can't place it. Who is the Manalonga pretending to be?

Primo, can you hear me?

It is sweet and delicate, this voice, almost like a song, and more beautiful than any voice he has ever heard.

"Who are you pretending to be?" Primo shouts.

I'm not pretending to be anyone, the voice says. *It's just me—the Manalonga.*

The blood in Primo's body runs cold.

I heard you found my ring, Primo. That's wonderful news! You are quite right about its power, too. We can't hurt you while you have it hanging around your neck. I just so want to see my beautiful ring again! Would you please come to the edge so I can see it? Just a bit closer?

Primo feels the sweat glaze his palms. He gulps. Is this *really* a good idea?

He takes a second step.

Don't worry! You'll be fine, Primo. I'm not a terrible monster or anything. Not that it even makes a difference. After all, you and I both know I can't hurt you while you have my ring.

Can it be lying?

Of course it can be lying! That's what Manalonga do—they lie!

It is agony, to wait there one step away. Primo feels like he is in a nightmare he can't wake up from. He looks back to the others. They are calling to him, but he can't hear them, not over the roar of the water and the sweet coaxing voice of the Manalonga.

Now the Manalonga begins to sing a beautiful tune. Primo can't understand the words, or even what language they're in. He touches the ring, for strength, but it doesn't feel hot with power. It feels cold and dead against his chest.

But this is not the moment to be a coward. Primo screws up his courage and takes that final step. He leans over the edge . . .

And feels himself get hit by something. Then again. Now he is getting pelted.

A thunderclap sounds, and Primo realizes what is hitting him: hail! The icy balls pound the bridge like rifle shots and roll down its slopes like marbles.

Suddenly, Primo feels Isidora grabbing him by the arm and pulling him down the ramp of the bridge. Then they start running with the other kids through the battering hail to take cover in the watchtower.

Primo laughs uncontrollably the whole way there, and is still laughing when they get inside. That's when Isidora slaps him square across the face. Hard!

"Wasn't one of you getting snatched by a witch today enough for you, Primo!?" Isidora's voice loudly echoes off the walls.

"If bravery equaled smarts," Emilio says, shaking his head, "then you'd be a genius."

Maria Beppina comes in just then, the last one running, as usual. She throws her arms around Primo.

"Bravery **is** genius," Maria Beppina says into Primo's ear. "And so are you!"

She is hugging him so hard it actually hurts.

11
TARANTELLA PARTY

FURNITURE is being moved out into the street from the apartment. First comes Isidora with a chair, then Momma with a pot, Nonna Jovanna with a stool, Maria Beppina with another chair, and Primo and Poppa with the table.

"Hey, what's going on?" Sergio yells down from his window across the side street.

"It's a party!" Primo yells up.

The band arrives, straight off the coach from Naples. As they warm up, Poppa grabs Momma and pulls her into the middle of the now-empty room to have the first dance. She is grumpy about the party. Who on earth would pay for a band when they can't afford clothes? Still, when Poppa starts doing his silly hop, Momma can't help but laugh and do the tarantella, too.

The sounds of the hammers and saws of men working in the alleys stop early. People from all over the Triggio start to trickle—then stream—in. The party wasn't supposed to start until the evening bell, but it has started anyway. On the way in the door, the men slap Primo on the back and the ladies pinch his cheek.

It's the first hot day of the year outside and even hotter inside with all the bodies packed in. The music and chatter are so loud it's hard to hear, but who cares? Everyone wants to celebrate—the long Janara season is finally over, and spring has taken root.

Primo is happy for the party. For three days, he hasn't been able to stop thinking about what happened on the bridge. Did the ring protect him against the Manalonga by magically making it hail? Or was that just dumb luck?

Primo also keeps thinking about Maria Beppina. The way she held him so tightly—was she really that afraid of something happening to him? When she got caught by the Clopper, he had been more worried about his ring than Maria Beppina. It makes Primo feel like a jerk. But he was always kind of a jerk to her. Which makes him just feel bad.

He also feels like a fraud. *Bravery is genius!* Maria Beppina said to him, but she is the one who stood up to a witch. *And* escaped!

Everyone is clapping and stomping and taking turns dancing. That is, everyone is taking turns dancing with Poppa. Primo goes to where Maria Beppina is talking with the Twins, and as he does, Poppa pulls them all into the center, Primo to dance with Rosa and Maria Beppina with Emilio. (Sergio, seeing what is happening, hurries to hide. He hates to dance.) Primo and Rosa don't so much dance as try to outdo each other, while the other two try their best to stay out of the way. Then it is time to switch partners and Primo is with Maria Beppina.

As they dance, Primo leans toward her ear. "You're the brave one, cousin, not me!" he says.

Maria Beppina blushes. She then seems about to tell him something, but Poppa cuts in and starts dancing with her.

Primo wonders what she was going to say, and he means to ask her, but with so much else going on at the party, he forgets.

Our book is done, but life goes on!

SO, maybe bravery is not such a bad thing after all. At least, not so bad when you have good friends and family and a little bit of luck.

But what of these family and friends? Are they all telling Primo the truth? Do they have secrets of their own? Don't you just _wish_ you could go inside their heads and find out what they are REALLY thinking?

Oh wait, you can!

Lucky reader—you have more books awaiting you. And you MUST read them, because don't you need to know whether or not Rosa actually stopped the Janara? (I believe her twin brother sees things rather differently!) And what really happened when the Clopper snatched Maria Beppina? What was she about to tell Primo, anyway?

Sigismondo
RAFAELLA
BRUNO

S.   R.   B.

WITCHONARY

IN Benevento, any kind of supernatural being is called a witch. And boy, are there a *lot* of them.

The Clopper: An old witch believed to be the last of her particular kind. She haunts the open square of the Theater, chasing children who dare cross it. Every kid in Benevento knows the *clop clop clop* of her one wooden clog!

Demons: Wily magical creatures who live among humans disguised as animals. In Benevento, 1 in 7 cats are demons, unless they are black, in which case it's 2 out of 3. Dogs, on the other hand, are never demons. Goats almost always are.

Ghosts: Spirits of those who died before their time. They must be taken care of by the descendants in whose homes they dwell. (Also called Ancestor Spirits.)

Goblins: Animal-like creatures whom Janara often keep as pets.

Janara: (Juh-NAHR-uh) Certain men and women can transform themselves into this type of witch by rubbing a magic oil into their armpits and saying a spell, after which they fly off to their famous tree to start a night of mischiefs. Janara belong to a secret society and don't dare reveal their secret identities to anyone!

Manalonga: (Man-uh-LONG-uh) The most feared of all witches. They lurk under bridges or inside wells and try to snatch children for unknown (but surely sinister) purposes.

Mares: A type of goblin who sits on children's chests at night, causing bad dreams.

Spirits: Witches who have no earthly bodies and live in one particular place, be it a house, chimney, stream, or arch. Types of spirits include ghosts, house fairies, and water sprites.

Life was very different in Benevento in the 1820s.
HERE'S HOW THEY LIVED.

❖ Kids didn't go to school, they worked. They still *learned*; it was just how to be a craftsman, like a baker or a candlemaker.

❖ Could kids read? No way! Not many of them, anyway. Their parents couldn't read either. Reading was considered weird.

❖ Shoes were only for fancy people.

❖ There was a lot of dirt. Roads were dirt. The floor of most homes was dirt.

❖ Most people never lived anywhere but the home they were born in. Some never left the town they were born in. Not even once.

✧ Telling time was totally different then. Mostly, you listened for bells—the dawn bell, the work bell, the noon bell. But if you lived outside of town, you told time by the sun (and maybe the crow of the rooster).

✧ There was no electricity. For light, you used a candle or an oil lamp.

✧ Houses didn't have water, either. To get some, you needed to take a bucket to a well or fountain. To wash clothes, you went to the river. Oh, and if you needed to use a toilet, you had to go outside for that, too!

If you want to learn MORE, please visit www.witchesofbenevento.com.

HISTORICAL NOTE

THE WITCHES OF BENEVENTO is set in 1820s Benevento.

Benevento was an important crossroads in Roman times and was the capital of the Lombards in Southern Italy during the early Middle Ages.

Even before the Romans conquered it, the town was famous as a center of witches. (Its original name, Maleventum—"bad event"—was switched by the Romans to Beneventum—"good event"—in hope of changing things. It didn't work.) For hundreds of years, Benevento was believed to be the place where all the witches of the world gathered, attending their peculiar festivals at a walnut tree near the Sabato River.

The people of Benevento, however, never believed there was anything wrong with witches, and maybe that's why they had—or thought they had—so many of them.

JOHN BEMELMANS MARCIANO

I grew up on a farm taking care of animals. We had one spectacularly nice chicken, the Missus, who lived in a stall with an ancient horse named Gilligan, and one rooster, Leon, who pecked our heads on our way home from school. Leon, I have no doubt, was a demon. Presently I take care of two cats, one dog, and a daughter.

SOPHIE BLACKALL

I've illustrated many books for children, including the Ivy and Bean series. I drew the pictures in this book using ink made from black olives and goat spit. I grew up in Australia, but now my boyfriend and I live in Brooklyn with a cat who never moves and a bunch of children who come and go like the wind.

Read the other books in the

WITCHES of BENEVENTO
series!

MISCHIEF SEASON:
A Twins Story

Emilio and Rosa are tired of all the nasty tricks the
Janara are playing when they ride at night making
mischiefs. Maybe the fortune-teller Zia Pia will
know how to stop the witches.

Coming Soon!

BEWARE THE CLOPPER!
A Maria Beppina Story

Maria Beppina, the shy little tagalong, is always
afraid that the Clopper, the old witch who chases the
children, will catch her. And then one day she decides
to stop—just stop—and see what the Clopper will do.

Coming Soon!

RESPECT YOUR GHOSTS:
A Sergio Story

Sergio is in charge of the ancestor spirit who lives
upstairs. Unfortunately, the many, many demands of the
ghost make it impossible for Sergio to keep him happy.